Butterfly Brain

First published in Great Britain in 2020 by
PICCADILLY PRESS
80–81 Wimpole St, London W1G 9RE
www.piccadillypress.co.uk

A CIP catalogue record for this book is available from the British Library.
ISBN: 978-1-848-12868-2
Also available as an ebook
1
Printed and bound in China

Piccadilly Press is an imprint of Bonnier Books UK
www.bonnierbooks.co.uk

Butterfly Brain

Laura Dockrill &
Gwen Millward

Piccadilly
PRESS

For Jenny

L. D.

To Mum

G. M.

This might seem to you like an ordinary story.

You might even think that stories are boring . . .

but this is not like other stories – no!

THIS is a warning –

a tale of caution

that is rather strange and sort of gory.

It begins with a little boy whose name was Gus,
which was actually short for Asparagus.
He was one of those kids who always made a fuss
and stood out for acting kind of tough.

See, Gus was always getting told off
for **this** or **that** or **which** or **what**,
for starting scuffs and playing rough.
He never listened when Miss said —

ENOUGH
is
ENOUGH!

He'd just open his mouth and shout –

Teachers didn't scare him, nor did the rules.
He thought he was in charge, boss of the school.
He gave it the BIG'UN! and thought it looked cool
to make little kids tremor, squish big kids SMALL.
And there was one thing Gus always did without care,
something that someone like you wouldn't dare.
Something quite naughty, for which Gus had a flare . . .
The little boy was an expert at leaning back on his chair.

Said his teacher, 'I've told you once, I've told you twice,
it isn't funny and it isn't nice,
now ONCE again, SURPRISE, SURPRISE,
I'll tell you, Gus, this one last time . . .
STOP LEANING BACK
ON YOUR CHAIR!'

And dinner at home with his dad and gran
never seemed to go to any sort of plan.
Gus would spit venom like hot oil from a pan
and lean back on his chair with a
BANG,
BANG,
BANG!

STOP LEANING
BACK ON YOUR
CHAIR!

STOP LEANING
BACK ON YOUR
CHAIR!

I don't care!

I don't care!

I do what I want, SO THERE!

And you can't stop me, MEH, MEH, MEH!

I will ALWAYS, ALWAYS

lean back on my chair.

Then Gran said, 'One of these days you'll crack your head,
and, Gus, you'll be a sorry boy then.
Where hair once grew shall be stitches instead.
You'll be lucky, dear, if you don't end up dead!
Just imagine cracking your head at school!
If you MUST wear a scar then let it be for something cool,
like saving a cute dog or a bungee-jump fall – not by doing
something stupid, not by acting the fool.'

'WHATEVER!' said Gus.

'You aren't immortal, you are still a human being.
You have just one brain that holds all of your feelings,
all of your secrets, your ideas and meanings.
Your brain is your home and your skull is the ceiling –
and nobody wants a crack in their ceiling now, do they?'

11

I don't care!
I don't care!
I do what I want, SO THERE!
And you can't stop me, MEH, MEH, MEH!
I will ALWAYS, ALWAYS
lean back on my chair.

'Well, just you be warned, Asparagus dear,
your brain is more precious than a lean on a chair.
Life can surprise you as quick as a spear,
and swap rainbows with storm clouds and happiness with tears.
You are not a bad boy, Gus, this isn't you.
I know you get upset and angry – sometimes I do too,
but there's no need to lash out and do the things you do.
It's OK to just be you, you know. You have nothing to prove.'

But did Gus listen?
NO! NO! NO!
'You don't know anything, you old boot!'

13

It was like he was trapped in some hideous curse
and at school his learning only seemed to get worse.

15

Blood dotted the floor in a trail of red crumbs
and stained the soles of shoes like spat-out chewed gum.
Kids in class were frightened, crying –
'DADDY! MUM!
There's a kid at school today whose head exploded like a bomb!
And grey brain bits went everywhere like rancid sausage meat
and all this gunge snot stuff slopped blobs on our feet,
and there was screaming as his bone all crumbled like wheat!
All because little Gus couldn't sit straight up in his seat!'

You might be thinking, whatever, big deal, YOLO, that's all right,
it's just a crack to the head and if you're not dead, then fine.
It's just a bit of blood, you know, the scab will heal with time –
but no, no, a crack from leaning back doesn't just change your head . . .
it can also change your mind . . .

Just a crack,
just a crack,
from the front down to the back.
Just a crack,
fancy that,
from leaning a little too far back.
Just a crack,
a whack-a-smack-splat!
All gunge and blood and brain-head-fat.
A CRACK! A CRACK! A CRACK!

The crack
soon became a gap,
that you could not hide with a backwards cap
or even lovely crisscross plaits.
A crack that you COULD NOT stick back –
A CRACK! A CRACK! A CRACK!
Now it's wrong – it's going bad!
Now his mind is going mad,
flooding like a broken tap,
that won't stop dripping, *SPLAT SPLAT SPLAT*,
spilling out thoughts like mice from traps.
There was no chance for Gus to look back
and say, I REALLY WISH I HAD NOT DONE THAT!

Out went Gus's dreams, out went his feelings,
drifting like smoke into the pockets of the ceiling;
all he understood, all his knowledge and meaning
was now in the open air where everyone could see them . . .

The doctor was not best pleased . . .

'This is the silliest thing I've ever seen,
all your brain springing out
like a pack of jumping jelly beans.
And what shall we do with your empty skull now, eh?
Fill it with strawberry jam and buttercream?
You'll be lucky if you can think again, my friend, let alone dream!
But now you'll have to stay home,
for you, boy, have a SERIOUS case of –

NAUGHTY CHILD SYNDROME!'

Gus thinks he's the innocent victim.

'Can everybody STOP telling me off? I was involved

in a TERRIBLE, TRAUMATIC ACCIDENT!'

'Accident, smaccident!' the doctor continued.
'This is ALL your fault and it's going to be painful.
We have to sew you up with a thread and needle.
Now, sit still, won't you?'

THIS DOCTOR WAS EVIL.

Knots stitched Gus's skin and the PAIN WAS DREADFUL.

'Now, you're lucky we got here before ALL your brain fell out.
See, thoughts are private kinds of things
you don't want floating around –
ooooh, look, there's one of your ideas here splattered on my blouse.
It looks a bit like sad scrambled egg . . .
OH DEAR, THE CHILD'S PASSED OUT!'

Now here lies Gus back home in his sick bed,
spoon-fed, comic read, a bandage on his head.

But he heard the sound of night-time creatures,
leaves scuttling in the air –
Gus crept towards the window . . .

'HELLO?

Who's there? HELLO?'

Gus called out into the swollen night.
His tiny voice echoed and gave him a fright.
The moon was a smiling coin, a face shining bright,
but something did not feel normal . . . no . . . something wasn't right.
Stillness. Silence. Then again a –
RAT-A-TAT-TAT!

But all Gus received was the rattle of the breeze,
the humming of the leaves and the chatter of the trees.
It must've been a nightmare . . . from eating too much cheese.
There was one recurring fear that appeared in Gus's dreams,
one that made him wake wet with sweat and stuck to panic sheets:
it was the face of the gravedigger that he couldn't un-see,
that day his world fell apart and washed out to sea.

Could it be him now, the Maggot Man, to take him from his bed?
To drag him from his cosy home to live with the insects?
And then it suddenly hit Gus *SMACK* right there on the head:
did he survive his fall at all or was he well and truly dead?

NO.
This was real. It was just that Gus had lost
all of his memories; his dreams now he'd forgot,
his ideas and knowledge out in the air to rot –
but this he would uncover once he recovered from the shock.

Gus hid into the den of his bed, curled up like a prawn.
He was overtired, wired, and gave a giant yawn.

Until . . .

Gussssss . . .   *Gussssss . . .*

Gus leapt up in a pounce,
wincing in pain.
In a panic, flustered, he looked around the room . . .

Gussssss . . .

Gussssss . . .

The sound swirled and swooped.

Gus's heart was drumming with a *POUND POUND POUND*,
as he called for the sound
but the sound could not be found.
In one brave bound Gus leapt from the ground,
and switched on the light –

but then the light was put out . . .

'What are you? Some kind of weird ghost?

I can hear your wings . . . are you an evil spirit?

An angel?

Ohhhhhh . . . are you the ghost

of my neighbour's dead budgie, Gareth?

What are you?'

This is your little friend, this is your light,
this is your compass, your guardian, your guide;
these are your borrowed wings that nestle by your side.
This, Gus, is your very own brain butterfly.

She lives in your head, remembers everything you do;
your dreams, she collects, and secrets she keeps too.
If you're afraid, she protects you; holds you when you're blue.
She's brave when you forget to be; she takes care of you.

Emotions are full of colours, humans are made of shades . . .
Your butterfly flourishes when you do,
but cowers when you misbehave.
Sometimes, when you feel happy,
she lights up like a parade –

but when you are sad, or angry or bad,
she turns grey and shies away.
Just like she is today . . .

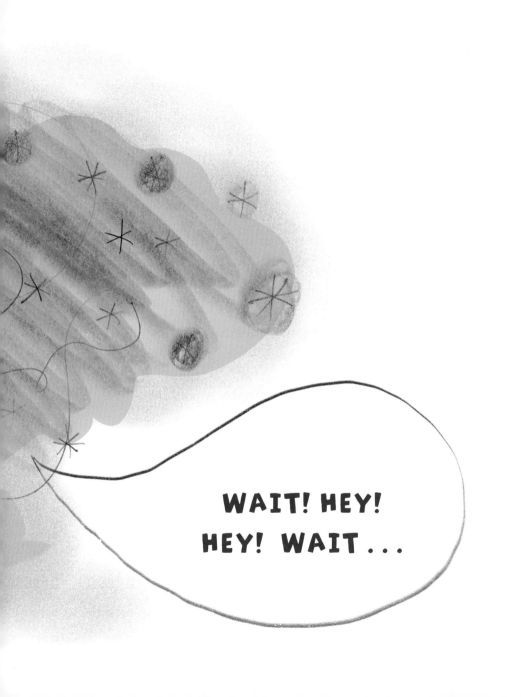

You made a crack inside your head, and that's how she slipped out . . .
Quick, quick, catch her now before she can't be found!

Out of the bedroom window the pair up and fly,
swooping silver loops into the night sky,
past popcorn clouds, the twinkling stars shine
bright in the night air, the planets magnified.

Imagine what a funny sight to go and pass you by:
a boy in his pyjamas and his brain butterfly.

Memories

The first stop was a crumbling, ancient hole,
stuffed in the depths where the moles might go.
It was gritty and dirty and brown and old,
it was muddy and stinky and damp and cold . . .

'What are we doing here?'

There were dinosaur bones, rotten missing teeth,
foreign objects buried down underneath,
where dusty books go and rusty hooks creak,
tangled in a fog to make your nose sneeze.

And lost in all that . . . were Gus's memories.

'It stinks down here.

Hey, I know you think I lost all my memories

when I cracked my head or whatever,

and yeah, sure, that's not ideal, I get it . . .

but do I even really need my memories back?

I think I'll be OK without them.'

'Don't you want to remember when you were five?
When you turned cardboard boxes into places to hide,
or when your birthday is and what food you like?
Well, dig deep, Gus, see what you find . . .'

'Yuck. I much preferred the flying bit.'

'Memories come and memories go,
quick as a heartbeat or snail-trail slow.
Some make you happy, some hunt like a shark,
some come unexpected like a bump in the dark.

'Memories come and memories go.
They dance in your head to your own disco,
and all you remember or thought you forgot,
is locked up inside your head's memory box.

'Memories go and memories come,
but take along the ones we love,
because people return, back and forth, to and fro –
but memories stick to you and never let go.'

'Fish fingers, snapping bubble wrap,
the cracked pink soap and the squeaky tap,
the hamster named Mr Flapjack
that bit your finger with a crack.

'Monday, Tuesday, Wednesday and then,
all the numbers up to ten.
Robots, seashells and nights in your tent,
ice-cream sundaes and letters sent . . .

'All the faces of your old friends
you remember now so don't forget . . .
your memories are safe and sound in your head.'

43

But just as they were leaving, the butterfly spotted a box . . .
It was sealed and worn and covered in moss.
'Does this belong to you? Is there something you forgot?'

'Nothing. It's not mine. I swear, it is not.'

'Are you sure? It looks like yours,
and it looks very big and very important.'

But Gus shook his head like he wanted to ignore it.

'You don't have any secrets, do you?' asked the butterfly.
Gus said nothing but his silence told a lie.

'Because this won't work if you're
holding something back . . .
We have to hold on to all of our
memories, even those that are bad,
because memories make us who we
are – they are all we have,
even the ones that frighten us, Gus,
even the ones that make us sad.
. . . No secrets?'

'No secrets.'

'Promise?'

'Making promises is weird and babyish.

I don't make ...

Fine, promise. Where to next?'

'Let's find out, three ... two ... one ...'

DReaMS

'Hello . . . hello . . . hello . . . ?'

This is the magic place where
dreams come to hide,
if you were ever thoughtless enough
to leave them behind,
lurking in the caves,
in the forest of your mind.
Most dreams we find are treasure –
some, not so . . . nice . . .

'Hold on, this isn't a dream . . .

This is a NIGHTMARE!'

47

OH NO! RUN!
IT'S THE MAGGOT MAN! RUN!

He once worked in the graveyard,
he buried down the dead,
but he is now the nightmare,
swilling in your head.
He carries a shovel,
he spits when he talks,
he hangs out with zombies,
that in the night stalk.
He terrifies the children,
and they made up a song
to warn others about him,
just in case he should come.

With a hunched back from his daily digging,
in the dead of the night you can hear him singing:
HERE HE COMES, THE MAGGOT MAN!
WITH EYES LIKE LICE
AND KNIFE-SHARP FANGS,
HE WRIGGLES AND HE JIGGLES
LIKE SPAGHETTI IN A PAN,
IN THROUGH YOUR EARHOLE
TO STEAL ALL YOUR PLANS!

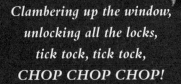

Clambering up the window,
unlocking all the locks,
tick tock, tick tock,
CHOP CHOP CHOP!

With a hunched back from his daily digging
in the dead of the night you can hear him singing:
HERE HE COMES, THE MAGGOT MAN!
WITH A GRIN ON HIS FACE AND A TONGUE LIKE SAND,
HE SLITHERS AND HE SLOBBERS LIKE WORMS IN A CAN,
BEWARE, BEWARE THE MAGGOT MAN!

Clambering up the window,
unlocking all the locks,
tick tock, tick tock,
CHOP CHOP CHOP!

With a hunched back from his daily digging
in the dead of the night you can hear him singing:
CAN YOU OUTRUN THE MAGGOT MAN?
HE HAS SPADES ON HIS FEET AND RAKES ON HIS HANDS,
HE SUMMONS UP THE GOBLINS,
UNEARTHS DEAD FROM THE LAND!
RUN FOR YOUR LIFE FROM THE MAGGOT MAN!

'I HATE THIS STUPID PLACE!

If that's the kind of dreams we've come to look for

then I don't want to do it.

Anyway, the Maggot Man is a nightmare,

not a dream. And it's stupid.

Dreams are meant to be nice. And he isn't. Not one bit.'

The butterfly, exhausted, fluttered around Gus,
her wings sparkling in the night air like dust ...

'But there are lots of other dreams too,
dreams I think might belong to you ...
of things you've always wanted to do –
be an artist, see the moon, do the world's biggest poo ...?

'There's a dream about a bed made of jam roly-poly,
an electric guitar, a vampire pony,
a wall made of fresh, pickable bogeys ...

'And then there's this other dream, sitting here, all lonely ...
I would ask you what it is, but I don't think you'll show me ...
and I can't get near enough to see it closely.'

'THAT'S ENOUGH!

Let's move on. I've got enough of my dreams back.

I don't want to see any more!'

'But this one looks special, there's something precious inside,
a dream I don't think we should leave behind.
We could open it up and see what we find –
we might see a face in this dream that you would like . . .'

'No! I told you. Leave it alone! Can we just move on?'

Imagination

'Around every corner is a second bend,
messages stored from bottled-up friends,
a whoopsie-daisy, am I making sense?
The clock's ticking backwards, am I Swedish again?
Your hair is a hedgehog, your nose is a screw.
Is there a vet about – my pet fly has flu!
My eyeballs are cookies, so my belly grew . . .
Is this where the imagination is? I don't have a clue.'

'I don't need no BORING imagination.'

'Everybody needs their imagination, Gus.'

'Duhhhhh. That's what computer games are for.

That's what comics are for.

That's what films are for.'

'That's what you think —
but imagine a world without a place to think.
Everything you know would vanish in a blink
and swirl like mouthwash down the sink.
Sure, we need seeds to begin fantastic-IN-isation
(I made up that word, copyrighted as of right now this second),
to dream webs with seams of inspiration
and wander the wonder of your invention.

'THIS IS HOW IT WOULD FEEL
WITHOUT YOUR IMAGINATION ...'

'I suppose having an imagination of some sort
wouldn't hurt . . .'

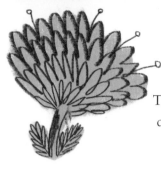

'I have a friend inside my head
I thought was just like me.
This little friend would dare me things
and say, "HEY, LET'S BE CRAZY!"
I tried to shrug off the little bug,
drown out its titchy voice,
but it would just shout LOUDER then:

"YOU REALLY DON'T HAVE A CHOICE!

"We are going to be quite wild today,
we're going to be quite stupid,
we are going to get up to naughty tricks
then act like we didn't do it!

"COME ON,
COME ON,
LET'S HAVE SOME FUN!
LET'S BEND THE RULES AND TROMP ALONG
THE CITY STREETS LIKE WE BELONG,
COME ON,
COME ON,
COME ON!"'

'My imagination saves me time –
when I queue up it queues with me,
it whips me off from standing in lines
and SCREAMS, "HEY, QUEUING'S SO BORING!"
Let's pretend we're pigeons today,
no, let's pretend we're goats!
Let's pretend we're superheroes
or have four hundred toes!
Let's pretend we own the world,
imagine we are free,
so close your eyes and count to twelve,
then run along with me!
COME ON,
COME ON,
LET'S HAVE SOME FUN,
LET'S BEND THE RULES AND TROMP ALONG
THE CITY STREETS LIKE WE BELONG,
COME ON,
COME ON,
COME ON!"

'But what's that still, small voice,
that strange thump in the night,
that moves all your toys about
after you've said goodnight?
That twitches the curtain,
and then creeps up the stairs,
that moves in slow motion,
and spikes up your arm hairs?
Is it really there . . .
or is it your own creation?

'Who can tell once you've shared
a thought with your imagination . . . but
COME ON,
COME ON,
LET'S HAVE SOME FUN,
LET'S BEND THE RULES AND TROMP ALONG
THE CITY STREETS LIKE WE BELONG,
COME ON,
COME ON,
COME ON!'

Gus and his butterfly were delighted with their catch.
All of Gus's emotions were safe and ready to take back.
'Just one more thing I have to ask before this task is through:
you don't have any secrets hidden, Gus, now, do you?'

Gus had a think and then shook his head.
There was that time he stole those crumpets and a loaf of stale bread,
the time he decorated his neighbour's shed with a box of rotten eggs –
but those weren't *reaaaalllllllyyyy* secrets,
he always got caught in the end . . .

'No. No secrets.'

The
Dead
end

'What's the matter?'

'We've hit a dead end,'
the butterfly cried as she fell away –
'I keep trying to push through, but there is no way.'

'What do you mean, a "dead end"?'

'There's something in the way . . .'

'In the way? In the way of what?'

The butterfly put in even more effort –
but breathless and defeated, she fell back.

'Can we keep trying?'

The butterfly was right, they had reached a dead end,
a wall from the floor right up to the sky, made of thick cement.
'Are you sure you have no secrets, Gus, nothing you're clinging on to?
Nothing you need to open up and take back home with you?'

'No, I told you.'

'Then I don't get it, it's all very weird.
Are you sure you're not holding back one of your fears?
I know it's hard and it won't just disappear,
but you must have a reason behind all those tears.'

'WHAT TEARS? I don't, Butterfly,

I swear I don't.'

'OK, I trust you and so I'll do my best
to get us out of this terrible dead end,
but you must promise to never again
do something stupid to your precious head.'

'I promise.'

But the butterfly twitched, her wings an ash grey,
injured and crooked and fraying away . . .
She slumped to the ground, panting on the floor.
'I'm sorry, Gus, I can do no more.'

'Huh?'

'I can't do all the hard work for you, Gus.
I can't help you if you don't help yourself. '

'But . . . but . . . wait . . .'

Gus panicked.

'Butterfly?

Butterfly?

'Please come back, Butterfly.

Please . . . I'm sorry, I'm sorry . . .'

And Gus could do nothing, only sit by her side
as the beautiful butterfly of his brain cells died.
And she slipped away and stole into the night,
and Gus felt the guilt –

for he had told a lie.

Gus did have a secret, his butterfly was right.
Imprisoned in a locked box that he daren't go inside.
It lay in the pit of his belly . . . but from time to time
it struck his heart, wild, clanged his bones with a chime.

But he didn't want to see it, he didn't want it to show.
It was his secret for the keeping, and not for anyone to know.
He didn't want to remember because then the pain would grow,
and where would his secret live then? Where would that pain go?

Secret

'I want to come and get you but I think I'm too scared.

I've blocked you out for so long

that I forget you're in my head,

and the idea of you will become the real truth instead,

to remind me that you're not here,

Mum, to remind me that you're . . .

'I can't do it.

I just want to go home.'

And Gus woke up, back in his sad little room,
troubled by the greyness of this endless gloom.
He didn't know what was what or who was whom,
only that his butterfly had left his heart too soon.

Gus read more comics, watched the day fade to black,
room-cooped, slurped soup, flat out on his back,
through the whole summer holidays like a pacing tiger trapped,
his heart hanging heavy in its cage, like an old potato sack.

The wallpaper had eyes, the stillness swarmed,
the slits in the blind captured stills of a storm.
Gus snuck out of bed, where it was cosy and warm,
because inside his head an idea had spawned.
Gus ran downstairs to find Gran and Dad.

'Dad. Gran. I've got something to say.

I'm sorry that I'm naughty,

that I don't always listen, 'K?

That I went and leant back too far that stupid day,

but now I've learnt my lesson. It's me who has to pay.

'I know that it's happened, I know what's done is done.

I know that I'm an idiot and that I've messed up.

I know you only tell me off

because I'm the one you love . . .

but I think I'm ready now. . .

'I'm ready to hear about Mum.'

'You were so scared that sad day, Gus. You were just a child.
You ran away from the funeral and out into the wild,
and the gravedigger found you and gave you a smile –
he said, "She's not gone, little one, she's just sleeping for a while."

'But you were so terrified, you said he looked like a slug,
said his eyes were crawling towards you like oil-black bugs,
and his teeth were shrouded in mud and so were his gums –
you called him the MAGGOT MAN and then shouted, "RUN!"

'You ran away from everything, you were scared of everyone.
But really you were running from the fear of losing Mum.
Gus . . .

'Your mum was interested in the whole wide world,
no matter the matter you could always tell
that even as a woman she had the soul of a girl,
as weightless as a feather, as light as snow fell.

'She was roaring with colour but gentle too.
She always knew what to say and exactly what to do.
She wore her heart on her sleeve but you were cocooned,
and when she died, we like to think she snuck inside you.'

'How to describe her? People have tried,
but she was as free as a song, impossible to define,
and if she was like anything, captured in time,
I'd say your mother . . . well . . . she would be . . . a butterfly.

'So don't let go, don't leave her behind,
don't let her be forgotten or fade away with time.
It's you who keeps the wings of your mother alive,
not just by remembering her, but by keeping her inside . . .'

'She's hidden in the numbers on your birthday cake,
in the flicker of a candle, in the un-tame flame.
You'll find her at the window, whispering your name,
in the mirror she smiles at you, through the look on your face.

'You'll find her in the garden, in the green grass,
tiptoeing on the edge of the water in your glass.
She flutters all around you and lands wherever you are,
and watches you growing from her throne up in the stars.

'Sometimes it seems like she's gone and I know that sounds hard,
but somebody who loves you never goes far.'

'For love never leaves you once you've known it from the start . . .

'For love never leaves you once you've known it in your heart . . .'